D0994444

Raintree is an imprint of Capstone Global Library Limited, a company incorporated in England and Wales having its registered office at 264 Banbury Road, Oxford, OX2 7DY – Registered company number: 6695582

www.raintree.co.uk
myorders@raintree.co.uk

Text © Capstone Global Library Limited 2021
The moral rights of the proprietor have been asserted. All rights reserved. No part of this publication may be reproduced in any form or by any means (including photocopying or storing it in any medium by electronic means and whether or not transiently or incidentally to some other use of this publication) without the written permission of the copyright owner, except in accordance with the provisions of the Copyright, Designs and Patents Act 1988 or under the terms of a licence issued by the Copyright Licensing Agency, Saffron House, 6-10 Kirby Street, London EC1N 8TS (www.cla.co.uk). Applications for the copyright owner's written permission should be addressed to the publisher.

Designed by Emily Harris
Art Director: Kay Fraser
Production by Katy LaVigne
Originated by Capstone Global Library Ltd
Printed and bound in India

ISBN 978 1 4747 9165 6

British Library Cataloguing in Publication Data
A full catalogue record for this book is available from the British Library.

The Pet Wash

A **PET CLUB** STORY

by Gwendolyn Hooks

illustrated by Mike Byrne

raintree

a Capstone company — publishers for children

Meet
the
PET CLUB!

Lucy

Jake

Buddy

Ajax

Lucy, Jake, Kayla and Andy are best friends. Lucy has a rat called Ajax. Jake has a dog called Buddy.

Kayla has a cat called Daisy.
Andy has a fish called Nibbles.

Together, they are the Pet Club!

Jake looks at his calendar.
The big day is coming soon.

Jake phones his friends.
They can all come over to
his house.

"It's almost Mr Carter's birthday,"
Jake says.

"We should get him a present,"
Andy says.

"He is our favourite teacher,"
Lucy says.

"And he helps us with the Pet
Club," Jake says.

"But we haven't got any money,"
Kayla says.

"Let's have a pet wash," Jake says.

"I'll bring a bucket," Andy says.

"I'll bring soap, combs and brushes," Kayla says.

"I'll bring my special pet-care
kit," Lucy says.

The next day, Jake puts a sign in his garden.

Andy fills the bucket with water.
Kayla adds soap.

"I think we should start by
cleaning our pets," Lucy says.

"That's a great idea," Jake says.
"You're first, Buddy."

After Buddy is clean, Lucy is ready
for him.

She is going to use her special
pet-care kit.

"Lucy, have you finished yet?"
Jake asks.

"Okay," Lucy says. "Here comes Buddy!"

"Buddy!" Jake shouts. "What has
Lucy done to you?"

"Don't worry," Lucy says. "Now Buddy can help us."

Soon Jake is too busy to think
about Buddy. The pet wash queue
is really long!

Finally, the last pet is clean.

"Our pet wash worked,"
Kayla says.

"And now we can get Mr Carter a present," Lucy says.

"Yes, we can," Jake says. "But I'd like my old Buddy back first."

"I think the old Buddy is already
back," Lucy says.

"That's my boy!" Jake says.

Join the Pet Club today!

Find the CAT!

Pets at the Party

The Lucky Charm

The Pet Wash